THE GRAND CLEAN-UP

Wax figures of various villains have come to life and caused quite a mess at the Ninjago Museum of History. Now the Elemental Masters are helping the curator, Dr Saunders, to clean up.

I LOST FOUR REPLICAS OF THE GOLDEN WEAPONS IN THIS CLUTTER! CAN YOU SEE THEM AROUND HERE?

TIME TWINS

These evil siblings want to gain control over time itself! But first, they will need four secret blades. They are aided by the Vermillion Warriors, an army of armour animated by snakes.

CONTROL OVER TIME WILL GRANT US IMMEASURABLE POWER!

Who are the twins? In each triangle, choose the letter with the darkest background. Read the chosen letters in each column to learn their names. Write the answers in the empty frames below.

SHALL WE BEGIN? LET'S NOT WASTE ANY TIME!

THE FORWARD BLADE

Acronix managed to touch Master Wu with his time-accelerating blade. Connect the dots below to find out what this dangerous weapon looks like.

I HOPE YOU WILL ENJOY LIVING IN THE FAST LANE, OLD MAN!

WHERE IS WU?

After being touched by the Forward Blade, Wu became faster than lightning. He's too fast to see, but there are traces left behind. Look closely and show Lloyd the one identical to Master Wu's portrait.

WHOSE TURN IS IT?

I'D RATHER BE DOING SOMETHING ELSE THAN CLEANING UP THE TEMPLE.

SAME.

OH! UNINVITED GUESTS!

WANT TO BET ON WHO WILL BEAT MORE OF THEM? THE LOSER DOES CHORES!

I ACCEPT! HERE GOES NUMBER ONE!

TWO FOR ME!

BUT YOU'RE CHEATING!

NEXT! I FORESEE SOMEONE CLEANING ALONE!

6

SECRET OF THE TWINS

The ninja have unmasked Krux! They can't believe he's been living in Ninjago City all this time. Do you want to uncover Krux's secret as well? Untangle the lines and discover his false identity.

THE NEW MASTER

Help Lloyd train with the other ninja. Arrange the Elemental Masters by filling the blanks with the right numbers. Make sure that no ninja repeats vertically or horizontally.

TIMELESS CLASH

Nya and Kai are facing the Time Twins to protect Ninjago City. This encounter may end in an epic battle ...

Look at the two pictures of this face-off and circle the ten differences between them.

STEEL AGAINST STEAL

Kai raced his bike through the streets of Ninjago City – now eerily quiet after the first wave of the Vermillion Warrior attack. With Jay, Cole and Nya, Kai had already faced his enemies on top of Borg Tower. They had even thrown a few off the roof, but the fall didn't seem to have much effect. Red snakes slithered out of the shattered armour and simply reassembled themselves into new fighters. And then the Vermillion Warriors had disappeared. But why? And where?

The ninja had jumped into their vehicles and raced off in different directions to find their foe. Their indestructible foe. "Hmm," Kai wondered. "Maybe sticking together would have been a better plan ..."

Kai suddenly spotted two of the warriors down a side street. He twisted the throttle and charged towards them. They were dismantling the steel frame of a new building that was under construction.

"Why did the builders have to use steel?" Kai said with a sigh. "Haven't they heard of plastic bricks?"

Kai jumped off his bike and into battle before the wheels had even stopped turning – and before he'd counted how many foes he was up against.

Uh-oh.

There were two more Vermillion Warriors on the next floor up, busy unbolting beams. It didn't take advanced ninja maths to work out that there were now four enemies in all.

But there was no backing out now.

Kai did Airjitzu upwards, hurling fireballs at a beam one warrior was trying to remove, welding it into place. Drawing his sword as he landed on another beam, he slashed at the warrior while it was still hopping around and blowing on its fingers, burnt by the searing-hot metal. The fighter crashed to the ground below them and shattered, with snakes slithering out of the wrecked armour ... and yep, slithering right back into the pieces again. The pieces wriggled towards each other, trying to reassemble.

"You guys give recycling a bad name," said Kai, leaping to the ground. The ninja narrowly avoided the giant blade of the second warrior on the upper level. His armour looked different – maybe he was some kind of higher rank.

"Yield, human!" cried the new fighter, jumping down to confront Kai. "Resistance is futile."

"Yeah, whatever," said Kai. "People are always saying that to me. And you know what? It never is."

"What never is what?" said the warrior looking confused.

"Futile. Resistance, remember?" said Kai. "Try to keep up."

Kai dodged the angry warrior's sword. "So are you the guy in charge here, or what?"

"I am Commander Raggmunk!" cried the warrior, circling. "And yes, I control these Vermillion Warriors with my thoughts!"

"Yeah? Too bad thinking isn't your specialty," said Kai. "Here's a tip: if you're going to dismantle a building, you don't start with the ground floor. Makes the floors above it kind of unstable."

"Are you calling me stupid?" roared Raggmunk.

"Yup," said Kai.

Raggmunk charged, but his fury made his sword blows rushed and easy to fend off. Now Kai attacked, forcing Raggmunk back.

Raggmunk touched a hand to his helmet to issue a thought-command to the two other warriors, while mouthing, "I am in need of assistance!"

The warriors dropped the beams they'd been carrying and closed in on Kai, surrounding him. Blow after blow rained down from their weapons. There was no escape!

"I bet you aren't feeling so smart now!" laughed Raggmunk. Then suddenly, he flew backwards, crashing into the beams of the building's ground floor to the sound of rupturing metal.

"Cole!" cried Kai, recognising an Earth Punch when he saw it. "And Jay!" he added, as a lightning bolt felled one of the other warriors. Kai's two friends ran to his side. "How did you find me?"

"We just followed the noise and flames," said Jay. "You sure don't like to fight quietly."

"That guy's lips move when he thinks," said Cole, nodding in Raggmunk's direction. "Did you notice that?"

As Jay and Cole tackled the other Vermillion Warrior, Kai rushed towards Raggmunk, who was staggering to his feet. But then Kai stopped abruptly – the whole building was starting to creak ominously.

"Guys!" Kai called out. "We need to get out of here – now!"

Jay and Cole didn't even stop to question him. "NINJA-GO!" the three cried in unison and used Spinjitzu to get out of harm's way in the nick of time ... just as the entire building frame collapsed on top of Raggmunk and the warriors.

The three ninja landed on a nearby rooftop and looked down at the wreckage. "My bad," said Cole. "My direction was a little off with the whole Earth Punch thing."

"Well," said Kai. "They did kinda bring it down on themselves."

Then they heard a muffled voice from deep within the tangled metal. It was Raggmunk: "This isn't over! Do you hear?"

"Wow," said Jay. "I guess the guy's too dumb to know when he's beat."

"Yeah," said Kai. "You might say his determination is steely!"

SNAKE HUNT

The Twins are using their combat armour against the ninja. Close your eyes and try to hit the snakes on the page with the tip of your pencil to block them from reaching the metal armour. If you manage to do it in 30 seconds, it will hold off the Vermillion Warrior's activation.

A MASTER'S WISDOM

As the new Master, Lloyd needs to prepare training for the ninja. He wrote notes on what each ninja should focus on improving. Match the descriptions to the Elemental Masters.

1. This ninja is too impatient. Assign queuing in lines.

2. This ninja should work on getting a sense of humour. I prescribe telling one joke per day.

3. This ninja is way too relentless. Suggest drinking more green tea.

4. This ninja's mouth just keeps jabbering ... How about reading books or listening to music?

5. This ninja has a lot of strength and will to fight. Recommend taking up gardening for some relaxation.

METAL THEME PARK

The ninja must reach the amusement park before the Vermillion Warriors take all the metal. Help the ninja through the maze as quickly as possible.

START

FINISH

EGGY AMMUNITION

Watch out! Vermillion Warriors are shooting at Zane from a catapult! Help the ninja knock the largest number of eggs out of the sky, before they hit the ground and release more snakes. Draw three straight lines starting at the crosshair.

LIGHTNING CYCLE

When the second Time Blade appears in the Ninjago world, time starts to slow down! Jay charges his motorbike, *Desert Lightning*, to hyperspeed to reduce the slowing effects. Mark two images that can't be found in the bigger picture.

A.

B.

C.

D.

E.

SPOT THE SYMBOLS

The Vermillion Warriors have stolen two of the Time Blades from the Airjitzu temple. But which one stole the precious items? Study the picture carefully and find the armour that has symbols identical to the ones shown on the next page.

QUICK QUIZ

See how quickly you can answer this quiz. Read the questions and choose the right answers.

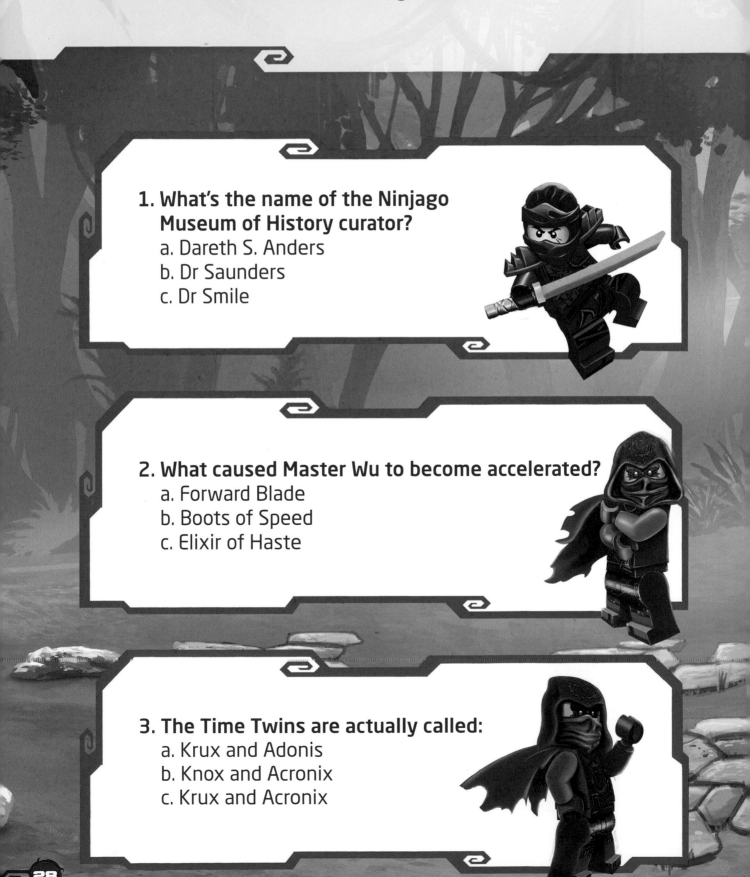

1. **What's the name of the Ninjago Museum of History curator?**
   a. Dareth S. Anders
   b. Dr Saunders
   c. Dr Smile

2. **What caused Master Wu to become accelerated?**
   a. Forward Blade
   b. Boots of Speed
   c. Elixir of Haste

3. **The Time Twins are actually called:**
   a. Krux and Adonis
   b. Knox and Acronix
   c. Krux and Acronix

4. What animals are Vermillion armour animated by?
 a. Spiders
 b. Lizards
 c. Snakes

5. Which ninja battled the Time Twins in Ninjago City?
 a. Lloyd and Zane
 b. Nya and Kai
 c. Cole and Jay

6. What special power does Jay's Desert Lightning bike have?
 a. Shuriken launcher
 b. Lightning strikes
 c. Hyperspeed

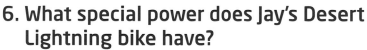

7. What happened when the second Time Blade appeared in the Ninjago world?
 a. Time slowed down
 b. Time stopped completely
 c. Time went backwards

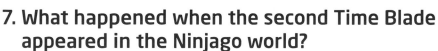

ANSWERS

Pg. 1
THE GRAND CLEAN-UP

Pg. 2-3
TIME TWINS
ACRONIX
KRUX

Pg. 8
SECRET OF THE TWINS

B.

Pg. 4
THE FORWARD BLADE

Pg. 5
WHERE IS WU?

Pg. 9
THE NEW MASTER

Pg. 10-11
TIMELESS CLASH

Pg. 18-19
A MASTER'S WISDOM
1 - KAI
2 - ZANE
3 - NYA
4 - JAY
5 - COLE

Pg. 20-21
METAL THEME PARK

Pg. 22-23
EGGY AMMUNITION

Pg. 24
LIGHTNING CYCLE

A.   B.

Pg. 26-27
SPOT THE SYMBOLS

F.

Pg. 28-29
QUICK QUIZ
1 - b, 2 - a, 3 - c, 4 - c,
5 - b, 6 - c, 7 - a.

HOW TO BUILD
THE VERMILLION WARRIOR

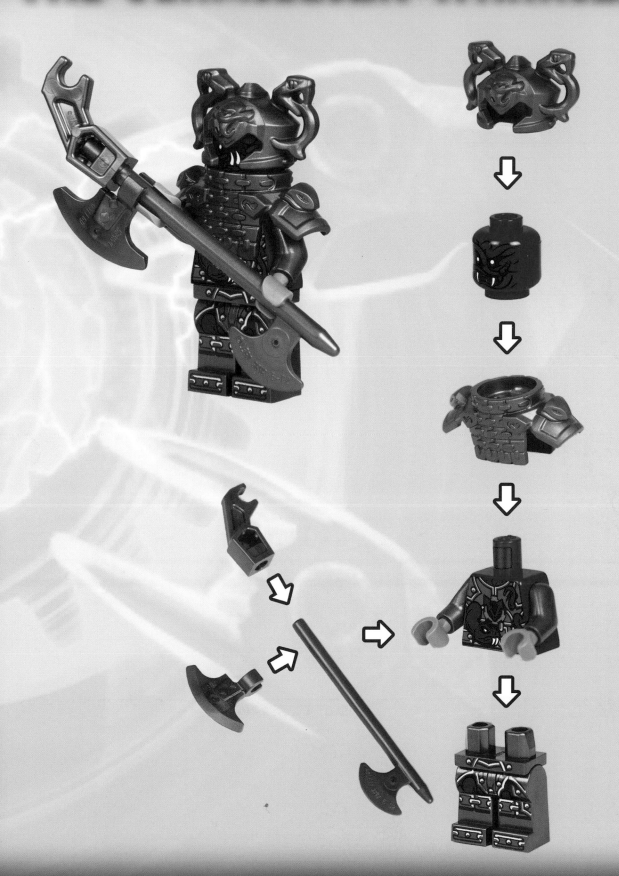